DATE DUE

JAN 0 6 2004		
JAN 0 5 2010		
JAN 0 4 2012		
DEC 1 9 2012		
GAYLORD		PRINTED IN U.S.A.

THE
CHRISTMAS STORY

With thanks to Dimitri and his parents

Copyright © 1996 by Kay Sproat Chorao
All rights reserved
Printed in the United States of America
First Edition

Library of Congress Cataloging-in-Publication Data
The Christmas story/adapted and illustrated by Kay Chorao.
p.   cm.
ISBN 0-8234-1251-2 (hardcover: alk. paper)
1. Jesus Christ—Nativity—Juvenile literature.   I. Chorao, Kay.
BT315.2.C54   1996   96-5066   AC
232.92—dc20

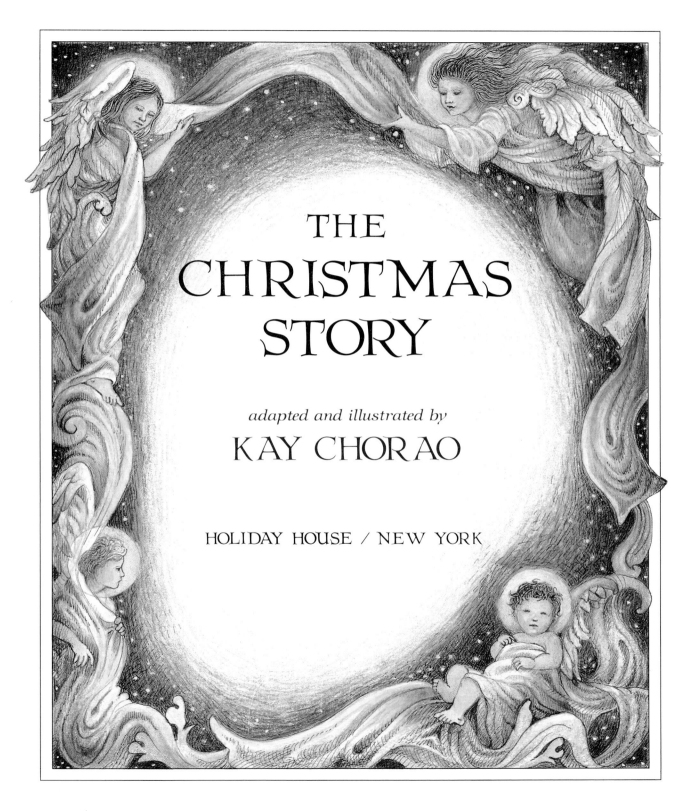

THE
CHRISTMAS
STORY

adapted and illustrated by
KAY CHORAO

HOLIDAY HOUSE / NEW YORK

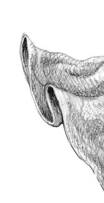

EARLY two thousand years ago a virgin named Mary was visited by an angel from God.

The angel told Mary, "You shall bring forth a son called Jesus, and He shall be great. He shall be the son of God."

And Mary said, "Look upon me, the handmaid of the Lord. Be it unto me according to thy word."

OW it came to pass, the Roman Emperor Caesar Augustus decreed that all the empire should be taxed. Each person must return to the place of his birth.

Mary and her husband, Joseph, set out for Bethlehem, the city where Joseph was born. Mary was great with child, and they traveled slowly.

HEN they reached Bethlehem it was crowded and all the inns were filled. So they found shelter in a simple stable.

Later that night, Mary gave birth to the son of God. She wrapped Him in swaddling clothes and laid Him in a manger.

 N the same country shepherds kept watch over their flocks by night. An angel of the Lord came upon them, and they were afraid. A wondrous light shone all around and the angel spoke. "Fear not! For behold, I bring you good tidings of great joy. Tonight the savior of the world is born. Go to Bethlehem, and you will find the newborn babe lying in a manger."

And lo, a multitude of heavenly angels appeared and sang, "Glory to God in the highest and on earth peace, and goodwill toward all."

HE angels left, and the shepherds said one to the other, "Let us go to Bethlehem and see what the Lord has made known to us."

So they left their flocks and went to Bethlehem and found Joseph and Mary, and the child lying in the manger.

The shepherds rejoiced and spread the good news among the people.

ARY held the child and treasured the glory of His birth in her heart.

T this time three wise men came from the east saying, "Where is this newborn babe? We saw His star in the sky and have come to worship Him."

When King Herod heard these things, he was troubled. Caesar had appointed him to rule over this land and Herod feared that the holy child might replace him one day. He asked the wise men to find the child. "So that I, too, might come and worship Him," he said. But his words were not the truth.

HE star rose before the wise men, and they followed it until it stopped above the small stable.

NSIDE they found the infant
with His mother, Mary. They knelt down and worshiped
Him, and presented gifts of gold, frankincense, and myrrh.

HAT night the wise men were warned in a dream that they should not return to Herod. So they departed another way. And an angel of the Lord came to Joseph in a dream saying, "Take the child and His mother and flee into Egypt." So they departed that night.

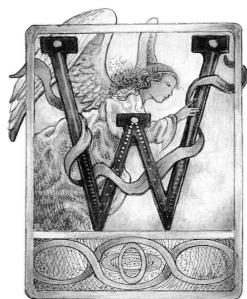

HEN Herod learned that the wise men had left his land, he was enraged. He sent his soldiers to Bethlehem to find the holy child.

Mary and Joseph stayed in Egypt with Jesus, until an angel of the Lord told them that Herod was no longer king, and it was safe for them to return to their homeland.

HEN they returned to Naza-
reth where Jesus grew with the grace of God.

The text in this book is adapted from the Book of Luke, 2:1–21, and the Book of Matthew, 2:1–12, in the King James Version of the Bible.

The pictures were inspired partially by such Renaissance masters as Murillo, Veronese, and especially Gerard Honthorst, but in some cases human models were used for the holy family. The final illustration of the child Jesus is framed by scenes from His later life: preaching in the temple, the catch of the fishes, the loaves and the fishes, the wedding at Cana, the healing of the blind man, walking on the water, and the calming of the storm.